First published 2004
by Black & White Publishing Ltd
99 Giles Street, Edinburgh, Scotland

ISBN 1 84502 018 9

Text copyright © Isla Dewar 2004
Illustrations copyright © Bob Dewar 2004

British Library Cataloguing in Publication Data:
A catalogue record for this book is available
from the British Library.

Printed and bound by OZGraf S.A. Olsztyn, Poland, EU

Rosie didn't see the purse even though it was slap bang in the middle of the pavement. She was spying on Mrs Winton who lived down the street and was going home with her shopping. Mrs Winton was always pretty grumpy. In fact, Rosie thought she might be the grumpiest person in the world. And at Christmas, she was grumpier than ever.

That was a thing about Christmas, which was only a few days away, that she'd noticed. It sometimes made people grumpy.

Like her dad when he took the Christmas tree lights out of their box and they'd be all jumbled up. A squirmy mass of knots with little bulbs sticking out all over the place. He'd start untangling them. But, when he undid one knot, another one appeared, then another and another. That's when his face would go red, he'd run his fingers through his hair till it stood on end and he'd start saying nasty things about Christmas and Christmas trees. He'd get grumpy.

Then there was her mum on Christmas morning when she had to get up at six o'clock to start cooking. Dad would come into the kitchen saying, 'Merry Christmas.'

Mum would say, 'Not when you've been up since dawn wrestling with a turkey.' She'd get grumpy.

4

Or when they went shopping and they'd have to drive round and round looking for a parking place. Then the shops would be crammed with jostling people, squeezing and shoving and trying to get to the counter to pay for the things they wanted. Everyone would get grumpy.

It was strange really, she thought. Christmas was lovely. It should be perfect with no grumpiness. There were secrets, surprises, wonderful things to eat and the telly was good, too. What more could a person want? Well, snow, she thought.

She'd had seven Christmases in her life and not once had it snowed. Not fair, she thought, it snows in my books, snows in the films, snows in the Christmas cards, but it never snows in Portobello. I want snow for Christmas.

That's when she noticed the purse lying on the pavement. She picked it up, turned it over in her hands. It was beautiful, dark, dark blue and covered with tiny gold dandelions. She took it home and showed it to her mum who was in the kitchen reading a magazine.

'What a lovely thing,' her mum said. 'I wonder who it belongs to?'

She opened up the flap on the side and read the label. 'Mrs Prudence Guthrie, 14 Lavender Street. That's just across the road. You must take it to her.'

Rosie took the purse to Mrs Guthrie. She wondered if she would get a reward. She knew she shouldn't be looking for one – a person should do things like returning lost purses because it was honest and kind. But, still, getting a reward for doing a good deed made her feel special.

Mrs Guthrie had come to the street a year ago. As soon as she moved in, a weird thing happened – her front hedges suddenly whooshed up so they were over six feet high. Now nobody could see into her garden.

When she was walking up the front path, Rosie thought this was a shame because Mrs Guthrie's garden was wonderful. It was full of huge blue and yellow and red flowers, birds sang and butterflies hovered in the air. It smelled of oranges, honey and something else. Rosie sniffed. Vanilla, she thought, that was it. Vanilla ice cream. All this was strange, because it was winter. And in winter, there's nothing doing in gardens. They are all bare and muddy.

She pressed Mrs Guthrie's bell and the sound of a thousand violins playing sang out. Rosie thought this a bit weird. But weird in a nice way.

When Mrs Guthrie answered the door, Rosie handed her the purse and told her she'd found it in the street.

'Why, thank you,' said Mrs Guthrie. 'How kind.'

Up close, Rosie could see that Mrs Guthrie was old, very very old. But her face wasn't wrinkly like a dried-up dishcloth. It was smooth with lines round her mouth from doing a lot of smiling.

'You've got a brilliant garden,' said Rosie.

'Yes I do,' said Mrs Guthrie. 'I like a bit of summer, don't you?'

8

Rosie said she did, but she liked winter because of Christmas. 'Only it never snows. It would be great if it snowed – deep and crisp and even like in the song.'

'Oh,' said Mrs Guthrie. 'I don't like snow at all. It goes for my bones – they get creaky and sore. I always make sure I don't get snow in my garden.' She smiled, thanked Rosie again for her kindness, and opened her purse.

Great, Rosie thought, fifty pence for me.

But Mrs Guthrie closed her purse again and said, 'What am I thinking of? You must have a wish. Go on, take one.' She waved her hand at a clump of dandelion clocks growing just beside the hedge. 'Help yourself,' she said. 'But be careful what you wish for. You know what they say – you might just get it. And don't be greedy. The wish department doesn't like it.'

Rosie went over to the dandelion clocks, picked one, thanked Mrs Guthrie very much and went home.

By now, Dad was home from work. The sausages were in the oven, potatoes boiling for mash, and they were both thumbing through magazines, waiting for everything to cook.

'Look,' said Rosie, 'Mrs Guthrie gave me a wish. I'd rather have had fifty pence. I think she's bonkers. She says it's always summer in her garden.'

'That's nice,' said Mum. 'She's not bonkers, she's just getting old.' Then, looking at a photo in her magazine, she said, 'How do you think I'd look with red hair?'

Dad said, 'Fantastic.' And, looking at a photo in his magazine, he added, 'If we had a boat, you could sit on the deck in a bikini while we sailed into the sunset.'

Mum said, 'Rosie don't go blowing those wish things all over the kitchen.'

She went to poke the potatoes with a fork, to see if they were soft enough to mash, but thought, dandelions in December? Strange.

In her garden, Rosie held the dandelion clock up to her lips, took a deep breath, closed her eyes, blew and wished. 'I wish for a perfect Christmas, no grumpiness. And snow. Lots and lots of snow.'

But there were still some wishes left on the dandelion, so she blew again. 'My dad would like a boat.'

There were still some left. She thought about wishing for a pony, something she really, really wanted. But remembered what Mrs Guthrie had said about being greedy. So she closed her eyes again, and wished. 'My mum would like red hair.'

This time, all the wishes flew up in the air. Some hardly went any distance before slowly floating to the ground. Some went as far as next-door's garden. Some flew up round her face and made her blink and sneeze. And some wishes, the ones she didn't see, drifted up and up, away and away, higher and higher.

'Wish coming in, Mr Plum,' said Daisy Starr.

'Not another one,' said Mr Plum. It had been a busy day. Christmas in the Wish Department was always hectic. He was looking forward to going home.

Daisy Starr, his wish assistant, wanted to get home, too. She was cooking lamb chops tonight – something she was rather fond of.

Mr Plum thought about leaving the wish for the next shift to deal with – the Wish Department never closed – and today, it being Christmas, had been hectic. Also, two hundred people in New Zealand had seen a shooting star, seven people in New York had caught a falling leaf and sixty-seven people in various spicy smelling forests across the world had stood in mushroom rings.

But he said, 'Might as well have a look at it.'

Wish number twenty-seven billion and six, he wrote in his huge book. 'Let's see,' he said. 'A perfect Christmas. No grumpiness. Red hair. A boat. And snow. Hmm.'

'Well that seems fine to me,' said Daisy Starr. 'It's not as if it's someone wanting a million pounds, is it?'

'But snow,' said Mr Plum. 'Snow's tricky. Everybody's wishing for it at this time of year. And the snow machine keeps breaking down.'

'Oh, go on,' said Daisy Starr, giving him a cheeky nudge. 'End the day with a tick.'

Mr Plum smiled, his cheeks went red, 'Oh, why not?' he said.

He put a big tick against the wish. Then Daisy Starr pinged the bell on her desk. The wish was granted. And they both went home for tea.

The next day, Rosie's mum said she had to go shopping and asked Rosie if she wanted to come along. 'It will be awful,' she said. 'The shops will be busy, and I'll never find a parking place.'

But Rosie said she'd go, even if it was awful.

In the Wish Department a red light flashed and a loud bell donged. Daisy Starr nudged Mr Plum. 'Grumpy alert. Someone's going shopping.'

Rosie's dad went to the garden centre to buy a tree. 'The Saturday before Christmas,' he said, 'there won't be many trees in a pot left.'

He was right. There were only four left and they were all ragged and sad. He bought the best one, though some of its branches were broken and it looked a bit thin and sorry for itself.

When he got it home, it looked even worse than it had at the garden centre. He sighed but set about getting it decorated.

In the Wish Department, the bell donged and the red light flashed. 'Grumpy alert,' shouted Daisy Starr. 'Tree lights coming out of their box.'

The lights came out of their box without a single tangle. And, as soon as they were plugged in, they lit up.

'Nice one,' said Rosie's dad.

He decided to put the lights on the tree, and leave the baubles and the tinsel for Rosie. But, once the lights were on, the tree looked even thinner and sadder. Only now it twinkled a bit. He looked at it and shrugged.

Rosie and Mum got home at three o'clock. They were in a good mood. They'd found a parking space right away. And, though the shops were busy, the ones they went to were empty so they'd easily found all the things they wanted to buy.

'Nice one,' said Mum.

Then she asked about the tree. Dad stared down at his feet. 'Um,' he said. 'I've got the lights on. But it looks a bit sad.'

Mum and Rosie went through to the living room. And swooned in wonder.

The tree was beautiful. It was suddenly
tall. And deep, deep green with thick long
branches, hung with coloured baubles.
It was lit up and dazzling. It no longer
just twinkled, it sparkled and glistened.
The room was filled with the scent of
Christmas tree – the best smell in
the world.

Rosie said, 'Ooooh.'

Her dad said, 'Weird.
Really, really weird. It
wasn't like that when I
left it.'

On Christmas Day, Rosie woke early. Her presents were at the bottom of her bed. Everything she'd asked for was there – a watch, a video of her favourite cartoon film, books, a new game for her computer. And, over by the door, a red bike. She was thrilled. She was over the moon.

But there was something else. There was a strange light in the room, a bluish light. Outside the world was hushed, silent. She went over to the window, peered out. It was snowing. Hundreds, thousands of fat white flakes were floating down, covering the house, her window sill, the garden.

Rosie ran through to her mum and dad's bedroom singing, 'It's snowing! It's snowing!'

Mum yawned, rubbed her eyes and said, 'Oh, Rosie, it's five o'clock in the morning.'

She sat up. 'Goodness,' she said, 'there's a huge boat in the room.'

Dad sat up too, rubbed his eyes and stared. 'Your hair's bright red,' he said.

Mum jumped out of bed, ran over to the mirror and screamed. 'It's red! A horrible scarlet colour. How did that happen? And how did that boat get in here?'

Dad looked at the boat. 'It's not so much a matter of how it got in – how are we going to get it out?'

Rosie kept on singing, 'It's snowing. It's snowing.'

Mum pulled back the curtain and said, 'She's right. It's snowing.'
Then she looked again. 'But it's only snowing on our house.'

Dad said, 'Rubbish.' Then he got up and looked out.

The rest of the street was dark but he could see that all the other
gardens were still exactly as they'd been yesterday and the day
before. Green grass, green hedges, muddy earth in the flower beds
and not a drop of snow on any of them.

Both Mum and Dad said, 'Weird.'

That's when the doorbell rang. It rang and rang and rang. Mum
said, 'Who can that be at this time in the morning?'

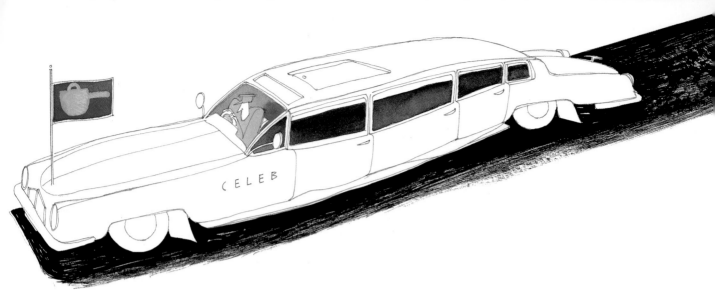

She put on her dressing-gown and ran down the stairs shouting, 'All right. I'm coming.'

Upstairs, leaning over the rail at the top of the stairs, Rosie and Dad heard the front door being opened. A voice said, 'Aha. Merry Christmas. It's me, Rory O'Gratin, come to cook your Christmas dinner. Your hair's an odd colour, if you don't mind me saying.'

Mum said, 'But . . .' Then she was squashed against the wall as people battered past her and ran into the kitchen.

'It's that celebrity cook off the telly – Rory O'Gratin that shouts at people and makes wonderful things,' said Rosie.

'I know who he is,' said Dad. 'But what's he doing here?'

They heard Mum shouting, 'Let me into my kitchen. I want a cup of tea.'

And the cook off the telly shouting, 'Nobody enters my kitchen when I'm preparing a feast. I will make your breakfast.'

Mum came slowly back upstairs. 'That cook from the telly chased me out of my kitchen.' Then she said, 'He's smaller in real life than he is on the telly.'

But soon they were all served breakfast – which was wonderful.

24

After that, Mum had a bath. Then she lay on a velvet couch while a team of pamperers did her nails, gave her a facial and rubbed her feet with oils smelling of orange, honey and vanilla ice cream. 'I don't suppose you could do something about my hair?' she said.

'No, madam,' said the head pamperer. 'Nails, feet, face and cushion plumping is all we do.'

The house filled with the smells of cooking and the sound of Rory O'Gratin shouting at his assistants.

Rosie went outside to play in the snow. She and Dad built a snowman. They had a snowball fight that ended up as a snow fight – they just lifted heaps of snow at threw it at each other. Then Rosie spent some time walking to all the secret places in the garden, making footsteps where no footsteps had been before. Dad would have cleared the front path but there was a small crowd at the gate looking in amazement at the only snow-covered house in the street. So he went upstairs to the boat in the bedroom and wondered about how to get it through the door, down the stairs and out of the house.

'A boat?' he said. 'How did a boat get into my bedroom?'

Word about the only house in the country that was having a white Christmas spread. Outside, the crowd got bigger and bigger so that, when Rosie and her family were eating their Christmas dinner (which was delicious, by the way, with a selection of four puddings), there were television cameras and reporters talking into microphones at their front gate. There were photographers standing on ladders so they could see over the hedge. Camera flashlights popped. There was noise, shouting, a hullabaloo.

But, by six o'clock in the evening, it was all over. The cook and his assistants did the dishes and went home. All the reporters, photographers and cameramen went away, too. A famous footballer had given his pop-star wife a diamond costing three million pounds and a politician had broken his toe and they were sure the world needed to know these things.

That night, Rosie and her mum and dad saw their house, covered with snow, on the news on the television. Weathermen were asked to explain how this could happen. But they couldn't. It was a mystery.

Before she went to bed, Rosie stood at the back door and gazed out at the snow. Stars were shining, everything glistened. She sighed, 'It's been a perfect Christmas,' she said.

Mum and Dad said, 'No. It's been weird.'

The next day the snow was still there. So was the boat. And Mum's hair was still bright red. Nothing changed on the day after . . . or the day after that . . . or the day after that.

By now, they were all fed up with snow everywhere. It was cold and damp. There was no room to move in Mum and Dad's bedroom and Mum said it was impossible to dust a boat. Dad had started to throw his underpants and socks on the deck at night because there was no place else to put them. Mum had been to the hairdresser three times but they couldn't find a dye that would change her hair back to its proper colour.

Rosie went to see Mrs Guthrie. 'Um,' she said. 'Sorry to bother you. But I was wondering if you could let me have another wish. Only, we're fed up of the snow. There's a boat in my Mum and Dad's bedroom and my Mum hates her red hair.'

Mrs Guthrie said she knew Rosie would be back. 'You don't just have to be careful what you wish for – you have to be very, very careful.' Then she told Rosie to help herself to another wish. 'And be careful,' she warned.

Rosie picked a dandelion clock, took it to her back garden, closed her eyes and blew and wished. 'Please make the snow go away.' She blew again, 'Please turn my Mum's hair back to its old colour.' She blew again, 'Please put the boat into a harbour.' She opened her eyes, there were still some wishes left. She could make another wish. Who could resist?

Next morning, she woke early and tiptoed through to her Mum and Dad's bedroom.

The boat had vanished. Rosie wondered where it was but she supposed they'd find it one day. There wouldn't be that many boats floating about with underpants on the deck.

Mum's hair was back to normal, too.

Mum will be pleased, Rosie thought. She'll be in a good mood, which will be handy when I tell her about the pony in my bedroom.